Walter Crane

A Romance of the Three Rs

Walter Crane

A Romance of the Three Rs

ISBN/EAN: 9783744658997

Printed in Europe, USA, Canada, Australia, Japan

Cover: Foto ©Andreas Hilbeck / pixelio.de

More available books at **www.hansebooks.com**

:PREFACE:

OF the three books composing this volume, which can also be had separately, "SLATE·AND·PENCILVANIA" appeared last year. It was originally intended to issue them to=gether, but it has not been found practicable to complete the set until now.

If my hobby-horses serve in any degree to help little folks over the rough stones of the road to Reading, Writing, and AR=.ithmetic, or afford pleasant pastime by the way, they will not have been ridden in vain. At any rate, if wishes were horses, this book should be, in the spirit of its cover-device, a Pegasus to all little passengers aspiring to run, and read, or write.

Walter Crane

Sept: 1886.

A Romance of the Three Rs

Penned & Pictured by Walter Crane

London: Marcus Ward & Co Lim?
1886 · Oriel · House · Farringdon S?

Printed by

Marcus Ward & Company Limited

Oriel House
Farringdon St.
London. E.C.

· LITTLE ·
· QUEEN ·
ANNE;
and Her Majesty's Letters
(Patent.)
Penned and Pictured by
· WALTER · CRANE ·

· LONDON ·
MARCUS · WARD
& Co. LIM'D:
· 1886 ·

A B C D E F G H I J K L M N O

Little
Queen
Anne,
sitting
as usual
in the
sun,

gets a letter.

It was an
invitation
from Three real
Royal Rs to
a Fancy Ball!

She takes counsel,
and a leaf out of her Fairy-
Godmother's fashion-
book;

and orders her coach,

Pages
in
waiting.

to the
guest·chamber
where she meets
some old friends

and is royally received by the Three R's

The Second—
a litttle
exercise;

and the 3rd
some slate
refreshment.

but she prefers a chat with Miss Muffet

And, for any spare attention she may have left, there are Three Sisters who speak in all languages.

Her Majesty's
Sleeping - Car
stops the way.

The
great Magician,
Signor Science,
lights her out with
his wonderful
Lamp,

and she finds herself back again in the garden, dreaming of many happy returns to the Three R's.

Pothooks & Perseverance.
or the A.B.C-serpent.

Penned & Pictured by Walter Crane:

London: Marcus Ward & Co. Lim. 1886

Percy Vere pensively puts a feather in his cap and fancies himself a knight with a plume :=

And the next page brings
him his helmet,
lance, and shield

With the assistance
of his squire of paper,
paste & scissors, Percy
fastens on his armour.

And · mounting · his · hobby · horse ·

He sets off at a good round hand gallop, tilting at rings.

And penning down everything that comes in his way

Till his career is stopped by a formidable barrier: his hobby horse refusing the jump,—

ercy is pitched into a dark ditch on the other side

Which transforms him into a black knight when, by hook or by crook, a friendly hand fishes him out.

And hangs him on the line to dry

Somehow he does not meet the approval of Academy critics, though he does not feel himself so black as he is painted:

But he takes a fresh plunge and,
turning over a new leaf,
in the eyes of a fair siren
he soon writes himself.

Coming up again with a Capital appetite, after a long course of pothooks and hangers, he is transported to find it is dinner time, feeling ready for any

mount.

And curled up with a comfortable C=

He·feels·he·has·made a pretty big D

He puts to sea again,

In search
of the
A.B.C. serpent,

as it appears to an excited fancy.

And after a good round hand to hand struggle

Percy black & puts him down in white, with a bold hand:

Aa Bb Cc Dd Ee Ff Gg
Hh Ii Jj Kk Ll Mm Nn
Oo Pp Qq Rr Ss Tt
Uu Vv Ww Xx Yy Z

And so, becoming a full fledged
penman, he makes light of
his letters, and brings
his tale to —

the End

Very early in life he was suited for a sailor

and, at the seaside,
has thoughts of voyaging.

and, taking a few necessaries,

and the result of their conference is

Composed principally of slates and pencils

and,
marching
in double
columns

to their King, who, being engaged with an addition sum in his counting house,

Dick is shown
into the parlour
where the Queen
offers him some
honey she has
subtracted herself.

and sends him into the garden to help the maid do multiplication on the clothes line;

till she receives a check from a little black-bird and a division takes place between them at her expense.

Transform-
-ation scene—
Dick thinks it
as good as a
Pantomime